ABOUT THE AUTHOR

D.J. Lucas

always wanted to be a writer. Today D.J. is one of
the most popular children's authors around.
D.J.'s books include *My Teacher's a Nutcase*,
winner of the Smartstart Award and *I Dare You*,
winner of the Bitread Book Award.

Sally Grindley

the acclaimed children's writer, is D.J.'s favourite
author. Sally Grindley says, 'I would do anything
to write as well as D.J. Lucas, even lock myself in
a cupboard with NO biscuits to eat!'

For Chris Haslam,
good on yer, mate!
S.G.

Visit Sally Grindley's website: www.sallygrindley.co.uk

ORCHARD BOOKS
96 Leonard Street, London EC2A 4XD
Hachette Children's Books Australia
Level 17/207 Kent Street, Sydney NSW 2000
ISBN 1 84362 690 X (hardback)
ISBN 1 84362 691 8 (paperback)
First published in Great Britain in 2005
First paperback publication in 2006
Text © Sally Grindley 2005
Illustrations © Tony Ross 2005
The rights of Sally Grindley to be identified as the author and of Tony Ross
to be identified as the illustrator of this work have been asserted by them
in accordance with the Copyright, Designs and Patents Act, 1988.
A CIP catalogue record for this book is available from the British Library.
1 3 5 7 9 10 8 6 4 2 (hardback)
1 3 5 7 9 10 8 6 4 2 (paperback)
Printed in Great Britain

Bravo Max

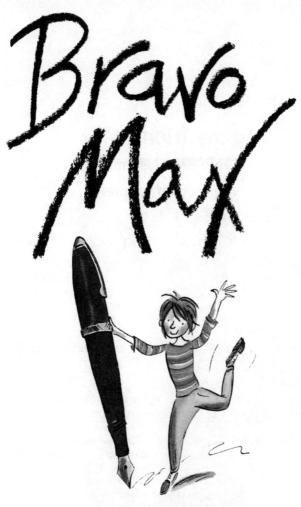

BY D.J. LUCAS
AKA SALLY GRINDLEY

ORCHARD BOOKS

To my friend Max

D.J.

Dear D.J.,

It's me again! Are you back from Australia yet?
I bet you missed my letters while you were
away. I had a great Christmas at Uncle Derek
and Pauline's. Their mad dog Scallywag stole
some of Gran's Christmas pudding when she
wasn't looking. Lucky it wasn't the bit with the
money in!

Thank you, thank you, thank you for your
postcard and for the signed copy of your new

book – *My Teacher's a Fruitcake*. I've already read it and it's just as funny as *My Teacher's a Nutcase*. I love it when the teacher falls into the sandpit and a dog eats her shoes.

Have you made any New Year's resolutions? I made one. I was going to try not to step on any cracks in the pavement on my way to and from school, but I forgot and trod on one on the very first day! Doh!

Love, Max

P.S. You're still my favourite author.

Dear D.J.,

I don't think you can be home because you haven't written, but I'm going to keep writing until you write back – so there!

You'll never guess what. You know my Uncle Twinkle Toes Derek and his girlfriend Pauline, well they belong to a theatre club and they're in a play called *Cinderella and the Beanstalk* and Mum and I are going to see it. I bet it'll be amazing because Uncle Derek's in it.

Have you ever written a play? When I told my teacher, Miss Dimmer, that I was going to see a play, she said jolly good because we'll be doing plays in class soon.

y up and write or I'll have to find a new

ourite author!

Love, Max

P.S. We've got a football match on Saturday and I'm in the starting team. YIPPEE! Huge Bigbottom was rude about me being in the team but he doesn't scare me. Just let him try!

21st January

Dear Max,

We're back. Phew! What a trip! Your two letters were waiting impatiently for me on the doormat, and I'm rushing to answer them because I don't want someone else taking over as your favourite author. Thank goodness you enjoyed *My Teacher's a Fruitcake*, or there might not have been any letters waiting!

We had a wonderful trip, Max. The highlight was walking over Sydney harbour bridge, which is so high it makes your stomach drop into your boots. I tried surfing for the first time, but I spent more time under the water making friends with the local fish than I did on my board. Christopher is a whizz at surfing, but he has flown to Australia lots of times so he's had plenty of practice. Now I must get down to some serious writing and thread all my research into my new story.

You sound really happy, Max. Well done for getting into the football team. Just you prove Huge Bigbottom wrong.

Love D.J.

P.S. I haven't written any plays, but one day... I just might.

Dear D.J.,

I'm soooooo glad you're back. It seemed like you were away for ever!

Guess what, guess what, GUESS WHAT! Uncle Derek and Pauline have got engaged and they're going to get married this September! And guess what happened. In *Cinderella and the Beanstalk*, Uncle Derek played the giant and Pauline was Cinderella. The best bit was when Uncle Derek sat in the biggest custard pie you've ever seen just before he left for the ball. He was soooooo funny, Mum had tears rolling down her cheeks. She laughed just like she used to before Dad died.

Anyway, right at the end, when Cinderella danced with the prince, giant Uncle Derek pushed the prince out of the way and asked Cinderella – well, Pauline – to marry him. And she said yes. And everybody in the audience cheered like mad. Mum cried again because she was so happy and said if Dad had been there he would have called her a silly daft duck.

Love, Max

P.S. I nearly scored a goal in our football match, and I'm in the team again this week. Huge Bigbottom never passes to me, but Ben does because that's what best friends are for.

This is a picture of Uncle with his big belly being a giant proposing to Pauline. Oh yes it is!

27th January

Dear Max,

That's great news about Uncle Derek and Pauline. What a dramatic way to propose to someone. Thank goodness Pauline said yes!

Love D.J.

Dear D.J.,

Seeing *Cinderella and the Beanstalk* has made me want to write a really really really funny play to make everyone laugh. And I like all the bits where the audience have to join in and shout things, especially when they have to boo the baddie. Will you help me with it, please, please, please? I promise to help you with your new story too, like I did with *Dear Max* (hee! hee!). When is *Dear Max* going to be published?

You haven't told me what's happening with your new story since you went to Australia to do research. Will it have kangaroos in it – BOING! BOING! BOING!

Love, Max

BOING

P.S. I've got a new friend at school. Her name's Emily and she's got really really really long hair.

4th February

Dear Max,

Writing a play will be no problem for a boy
with a big imagination like yours. You'll need
a good plot and strong characters, but the plot
will have to unfold through the words and
actions of the characters on stage, rather than
through description like in a story.

When you've thought about a subject for your
play, decide how many characters you are
going to have and write out a cast list, perhaps
with a line about each person. But don't forget
that you won't be able to fit too many people
on stage at the same time. They might topple
off or knock the scenery over!

I'm calling my new story *Where There's a Will*. It's about a boy named Will who is brilliant at surfing but has an accident which leaves him unable to walk. It's more serious than my other books, but it still has lots of funny moments, though no kangaroos so far.

Good luck with the play, Max.

Love D.J.

P.S. I don't know when *Dear Max* is going to be published, but I've just heard that a very famous illustrator called Tony Ross is going to do the illustrations.

P.P.S. Say hello for me to Emily with the long hair.

Dear D.J.,

I can't wait to see Tony Ross's illustrations for
Dear Max. I looked at some of his books in the
library and he's the best.

Mum took me out to a restaurant last night. She's
got a new job working in a bank and she wanted
to celebrate, even though she said it doesn't
mean we're going to be millionaires.

We had such a brillypants time,
D.J. The food was
delicious. Our waiter
called me 'Sir' and
made me feel like
a grown-up, so
when we stood

up to go, I said to Mum, 'Would Madam like to take my arm?' and she did. We walked all the way home like that, and when we went through the front door, Mum said, 'Thank you, Sir, you're a real gentleman.' I love it when me and Mum act daft together.

Love, Max

P.S. I've decided to write a play about George and the Dragon, except it's going to be called *Buster and the Dragon*.

P.P.S. How do I write my play out?

11th February

Dear Sir,

I understand Sir would like to know how to write out a play. He will be delighted to know that it is not a complicated exercise. He simply has to follow the example below:

MAX: I'm going to write a play about a boy who has to fight a dragon.

DRAGON: Will the dragon be fierce and scary but handsome?

MAX: The dragon will be the ugliest dragon ever seen.

DRAGON: Then the dragon will have to eat the boy before the boy can write his play!

(The dragon chases the boy, but the boy escapes. Smoke fills the stage as the dragon shows his anger.)

I do hope this will be of some help to Sir.

Kind regards, D.J.

P.S. You don't need to use speech marks, Max, and you need to put in brackets all the notes about who is doing what on stage and any details about sound and lighting effects.
Have fun!

12th February

Dear D.J.,

I can't believe your book *My Teacher's a Nutcase* is being made into a film!!! It said so in the newspaper this morning – Mum showed me.

Why didn't you tell me? It's my best book of all time and now there's a film – YIPPEE! Does that mean you're going to be a movie star?! You'll be an even more famous author than ever now. You will still write to me, won't you?

Love, Max

15th February

Dear Max,

I am on my knees! I'm sorry I didn't tell you about the film. I just didn't want to talk about it until I knew for sure that it would go on general release.

I was asked if I would like to write the filmscript for *My Teacher's a Nutcase* – which is a bit like writing a play. It's much more complicated though, and so different from writing a story that I threw my toys out of the pram and gave up. Someone else has written the script and they've changed lots of things – including making the teacher a man instead of a woman!!! Tom Trews is going to be the teacher, and Jennifer Aniseed is going to be the school caretaker!

I wouldn't dare stop writing to you, but I am disappearing under an avalanche of requests to do interviews and sign books, so don't tell me off if my letters are sometimes a bit brief.

Love D.J.

Dear D.J.,

I can't believe they've changed your teacher into a man, especially Tom Trews! And I can't believe Jennifer Aniseed is going to be the grumpy old school caretaker! Mum thinks it's really cheeky to change things like that and so do I. They should keep what you wrote because it was your idea.

I've thought about the beginning of my play. Buster will be at home having breakfast with his mum when there's a great roar outside and lots of screams.

BUSTER: Perfect toast, Mum. Can I have
            some more, please?
MUM: What's that noise? I thought
            I heard a roar.

BUSTER: Someone's screaming.

(Looks out of the window.)

BUSTER: There's a dragon running down
               the street, Mum.
MUM: Quick, Buster, hide in the
               cupboard. I'm scared.

*(While they're in the cupboard the dragon
comes in, steals some toast from the
toaster, fills the room with smoke then goes.
Buster comes out of the cupboard, is very
cross about losing his toast, and decides
that the dragon must be caught.)*

Love, Max

26

21st February

Dear Max,

That's a great opening to your play. I can just
see the dragon gallumping across the stage and
stealing Buster's toast. Comedy and drama all
in one go! Have you thought your plot right
through to the end, and do you know about
breaking it down into different scenes? Scenes
are a bit like chapters and can be used to show
a change of time or place, to move the action
on or to change its pace.

What else is that dragon going to get up to
and how is Buster going to deal with him?
I'm intrigued.

Love D.J.

P.S. You're right about Tom Trews playing the teacher in the film. He's not quite the mad middle-aged woman I had in mind!

Dear D.J.,

Uncle Derek has persuaded Mum to join his theatre club, even though she says she can't act for toffee and would turn to jelly if she had to stand up in front of people. Uncle Derek says there are lots of other things she can do, like making costumes or painting scenery. Anyway, Uncle's taking her to a meeting tonight because he says it will do her good to get out, and Pauline is baby-sitting, even though I'm not a baby. WAAAAHHH!

It's just started to snow. YIPPEE! I hope it snows lots, then I can make a snowman.

Love, Max

P.S. The bad thing about snow is that we might not get to play our football match – it's the third time I've been picked! – and Mum was going to watch.

P.P.S. Have you met Tom Trews and Jennifer Aniseed yet?

Dear D.J.,

You should see the snow, D.J. It's like an alien world outside. I keep thinking a spaceship is about to land – PLOOOF! Pauline came to baby-sit with that silly mad dog Scallywag. He kept trying to catch the snow in his mouth. Jenny from my class, who lives in our flats, came to help us build a snow monster. She keeps wanting to be my best friend again, but she's not always nice to me, and anyway, I've got Ben and Emily.

Mum said she quite enjoyed herself with those theatre people and asked if I would mind if she went again. I said of course I wouldn't, because I wouldn't, because I want her to be happy. She's a bit worried about going on her own though when Uncle Derek is away lorrying. So I told her she had to be brave, like me.

Love, Max

P.S. In my play, Buster and his friends are going to be having a snowball fight on a football pitch, when the dragon arrives and melts all the snow with his fire.

28th February

Dear Max,

No snow so far. Lucky you. I adore snowball
fights. My dotty cat Donut thinks snow is a
type of bird and tries to catch it. Ambush just
barks at it.

I love the idea of your dragon melting all the
snow, but it might be difficult to make it
happen on a stage without flooding the
audience! Just something to bear in mind...
Some ideas are great in stories, and can be
made to work in films using special effects,
but are a problem in the theatre.

I hope your football match wasn't cancelled because of the snow or an invasion of snow monsters, and that you scored a million goals.

Love D.J.

P.S. I haven't met Tom Trews and Jennifer Aniseed yet, but I'm going to watch some of the filming soon. I expect they'll be just as excited about meeting me!

Dear D.J.,

I can't believe you're really going to meet Tom Trews and Jennifer Aniseed. You must be the luckiest person in the whole world!

Mum's at her theatre club tonight. I've got a new baby-sitter because Pauline's at evening class and Uncle Derek is lorrying. She lives in one of our flats and she's called Mrs Burrows, but I'm going to call her Mrs Rabbits because she talks a lot. She keeps asking me questions, like what do I want to be when I grow up, and all that sort of stuff that grown-ups always ask. She's knitting and watching her favourite programme on the telly at the moment and I've got to be quiet, so I said I'd do some writing.

Our football match was cancelled but the snow has nearly all gone and it's cold and slushy and grey everywhere. Hope Mum comes home soon. Mrs Rabbits has started talking again. This is a quick picture of her before she comes to look at what I'm doing.

Love, Max

6th March

Dear Max,

Does Mrs Rabbits like carrots?! I used to have a baby-sitter who never took her hat off! It was a pale blue knitted woollen thing which she pulled down to her ears. I always wondered whether she had any hair underneath. Her name was Mrs Postlethwaite and I used to call her Bossy Possy because she was, and she smelt of cabbage.

Have you thought about how many different settings you are going to have in your play? You can change them every time you have a change of scene if you like, though it's better not to make it too complicated. If the scene changes take too long your audience will fall asleep.

I must go. I feel inspired today, so I'm hoping
to be able to hurtle forwards with *Where
There's a Will*.

Lots of Love, D.J.

Dear D.J.,

It's Mum's theatre night again. It's funny because she didn't look like Mum when she went out. She had new clothes on and her hair was sort of different. I said to her, 'Mum, you look like a film star,' and she went bright red and said, 'That's very kind of you, young man, but flattery will get you nowhere.' So I said, 'Will it get me as far as a bowl of chocolate ice cream?' and it did.

Mrs Rabbits is here now. Mum asked me if I liked her and I said that she asks me loads of questions that I don't want to answer and that she says I'm small for my age, even though I've grown loads and I'm not the smallest in my class any more. Mum said she's just trying to be friendly, but she should know that it's rude to talk about people's size, shouldn't she?

Jenny's just come round and Mrs Rabbits says she can stay for an hour as long as we're quiet so she can watch her programme on the telly. Jenny asked if I would be her boyfriend. Yuk! I said I couldn't because she's taller than me. Anyway I like Emily better (but that's a secret).

Love, Max

Dear D.J.,

Mum's out again. I wish the theatre club didn't meet every week.

I tried to be friendly to Mrs Rabbits. I asked her if Mr Rabbits was at home, except that I forgot she was Mrs Burrows and she gave me a funny look and asked me who 'Mr Rabbits' was. I didn't know what to say then so I told her I needed the toilet. Now I'm in my room and I daren't go out. It's just as well I didn't ask her if she had any baby rabbits!

She's just been in and asked if I want to do a jigsaw with her. I said I was writing a letter and she looked at me all funny and said, 'Well, you're a weird one. I thought it was all email these days.' I told her we haven't got a computer and she went out – phew!

I think you might get a lot of long letters from me if I keep having to hide from Mrs Rabbits!

She's come in again and said she doesn't like me being in my room on my own when she's there, even though I said that Mum doesn't mind. I suppose I'll have to go and do jigsaws with her, but all my jigsaws are too babyish. Boring, boring, *boring*.

Love, Max

P.S. Mrs Rabbits smells of straw.

18th March

Dear Max,

Keep your chin up, Max. At least you only have to put up with Mrs Rabbits once a week and then she disappears back to her burrow.

I'm giving myself a great big pat on the back at the moment. I've finished the first three chapters of *Where There's a Will*. My writing's running away with me so fast that I can hardly keep up with it. I wish it was always like that. Will definitely has a few Max-like qualities – brave, determined, cheeky – but not quite so handsome, of course. I'll have to make sure that Max doesn't creep surreptitiously into all of my books!

Love D.J.

Dear D.J.,

I scored a goal on Saturday and Mum was watching! Huge Bigbottom was the only one who didn't say well done, but Ben was so pleased that he did a cartwheel across the pitch.

Mum bought me a new jigsaw. It's got 1,000 pieces! That's the biggest jigsaw I've ever done, and the drawings of the animals are brillypants, especially the big old lion. I asked Mum to help me because I like doing jigsaws with Mum. (I don't want to do it with Mrs Rabbits!)

Mum asked if I minded if she went out for a drink tomorrow night with some of her friends from the theatre club. I did mind a bit because I didn't want Mrs Rabbits to sit, but I said I didn't mind and Mum gave me a hug and said Uncle Derek and Pauline had offered to come – YIPPEE!

Love, Max

Dear D.J.,

Guess what, guess what, guess what! Uncle Derek and Pauline want me to be a pageboy at their wedding! I'll get to dress up in a waistcoat and bow tie and I'll be in nearly all the photos. They said I'll be a V.I.P. – Very Important Person.

Mum's going to make my waistcoat for me. We're going out with Pauline soon to choose the material because she wants it to match Uncle Derek's shirt.

I've done a bit more of my play. This is the beginning of scene number two, after the dragon has been back again and all the village are terrified.

SCENE TWO

(In Buster's garden. Buster is sharpening a piece of wood and cleaning his frisbee.)

BUSTER'S MUM: Please, Buster, don't go. Stay and look after your poor mother. Your father's already been eaten by one dragon. Let someone else fight that horrible dragon.

BUSTER: It's no good, mother. I am the only boy brave enough to fight that dragon, so fight it I must or nobody will ever be able to eat toast safely again.

BUSTER'S MUM: Can't we just run away?

BUSTER: No, Mum. Running away is what
              cowards do.

Love, Max

P.S. You see, I remembered your book *Who's Afraid of the Big Bad Boy?* and what the girl said to the bully. You can't run away just because you're frightened.

27th March

Dear V.I.P.

I love the bit of your play you sent me. You've already set up the direction in which the story is going and introduced your main characters, which is important. You've had lots of action with the dragon frightening the villagers, now perhaps you could move to a new setting to see what the dragon will do next.

I was in a school play once. I played Briar Rosebud and I had to throw my arms round Prince Charming. My bracelet caught in the ruff round his neck and I couldn't pull myself away. We were stuck together! I got the giggles then and ruined what should have been a very romantic moment – especially since I had a big crush on the boy who was playing Prince Charming.

Love D.J.

P.S. Congratulations on the goal, Max. David Beckham had better watch out!

Dear D.J.,

Mum's gone to the theatre club and Mrs Rabbits is here. She's taken over my jigsaw and she's doing the big old lion. I wanted to do him, but she said it was too difficult for me. Then she said the easiest bit was the tree and that I should do that. I told her I'd rather do some writing, so she gave me that funny look again and shook her head. I couldn't help myself when she did that. I said, 'I'm writing to my friend who's a very famous author,' and she said, 'Are you, dear? That's nice.' I could tell she didn't believe me though, and that she still thinks I'm weird.

I thought she was going to do my jigsaw all evening and there'd be nothing left for me

and Mum, but she's watching her favourite
programme now so I've got to be quiet.
I feel like making as much noise as I can just to
annoy her, because she annoys me all the time.

Love, Max

P.S. It's the morning now. I've undone all the
bits of jigsaw that Mrs Rabbits
did, so now I can do the
big old lion myself.
So there.

3rd April

Dear Max,

That big old rabbit is certainly a pain in the
burrow. You'll have to throw yourself into your
play-writing when she's there and try to ignore
her. If only you could tell her to hop it!

I'm about to go to Milan to watch some of the
filming of My Teacher's a Nutcase. It's all very
exciting, and rather scary. Christopher says
I'll be fine, but I'm sure I shall say something
completely idiotic when I'm introduced to
the stars.

Love D.J.

Dear D.J.,

Mum's got a new friend. His name's James and he knows Uncle Derek because he is in the theatre club as well. He took Mum out for a drink last night, but I didn't see him. Uncle Derek baby-sat. Lucky it wasn't Mrs Rabbits because with Uncle Derek I could watch the football on the telly.

Uncle Derek says James is a very nice man and I asked if he was Mum's boyfriend. Uncle said that at the moment he is just someone who makes Mum laugh. I told him that I make Mum laugh too.

Uncle Derek makes all of us laugh. Pauline says he's like one of those balls with a squeaker inside only ten times the size and one hundred times as bouncy. When he was baby-sitting, he

took a ping-pong ball from his pocket and said
he wanted to play table tennis. He stood some
books across the middle of the kitchen table for
the net and we
had a dustpan and
a saucepan lid as bats.

You should have seen us, D.J.
I couldn't reach anything in the
middle of the table because I'm too short, and
Uncle Derek couldn't reach because of his big
fat belly. Uncle Derek smashed one ball so
hard that it landed in the butter dish – SPLAT!
And then he crunched against the table and
broke one of the legs off! We both got the

giggles and lay on the floor for ages, then we had to spend the rest of the evening putting the table back together.

Love, Max

P.S. I'm going to have a big fat knight in my play who's going to protect Buster's mum while he's away and stop her from being sad.

P.P.S. The table wobbles now.

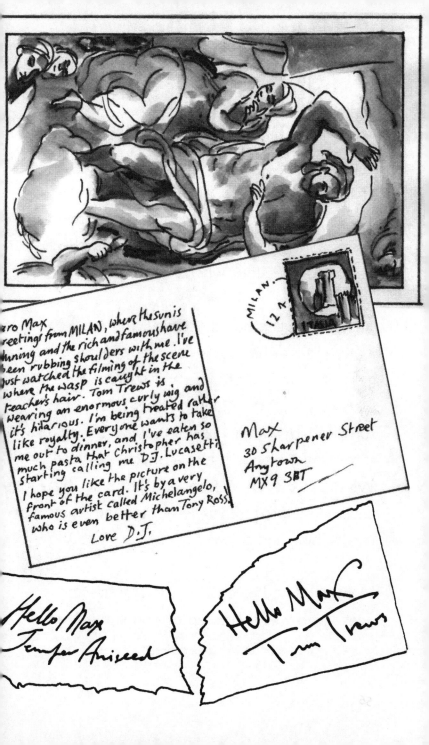

aro Max
reetings from MILAN, where the sun is
hining and the rich and famous have
heen rubbing shoulders with me. I've
just watched the filming of the scene
where the wasp is caught in the
teacher's hair. Tom Trews is
wearing an enormous curly wig and
it's hilarious. I'm being treated rather
like royalty. Everyone wants to take
me out to dinner, and I've eaten so
much pasta that Christopher has
starting calling me D.J. Lucasetti.

I hope you like the picture on the
front of the card. It's by a very
famous artist called Michelangelo,
who is even better than Tony Ross.

Love D.J.

Max
30 Sharpener Street
Anytown
MX9 3BT

Hello Max
Jumper Aniseed

Hello Max
Tom Trews

Dear D.J.,

Thank you, thank you, THANK YOU for my postcard and for Tom Trews's and Jennifer Aniseed's autographs. Everyone at school will be soooooo jealous when I show them.

I'm on my Easter holidays and I've been with Mum and Pauline to choose the material for my waistcoat and bow tie and to buy Uncle Derek's shirt. Uncle Derek wants Pauline to surprise him with it. I said it would be a big surprise if we bought him a bright red shirt! We didn't though. We bought light blue shirts and the material for my waistcoat and bow tie is dark blue and shiny.

Mum and I had lunch at Uncle Derek's and guess who was there...James, you know, Mum's

friend that I told you about. He's got a beard!
He wears a jacket with patches on the elbows
and he drives a silly old sports car. He's an
architect, but I don't think he can have much
money if he's got patches.

He's not as good at football as Uncle Twinkle
Toes Derek, even though Uncle's got a big fat
belly. He gave Mum a kiss on the cheek when
we left. Yuk! Fancy being kissed by a man with
a beard! I'm going to call him Hairychops.

When I said to Mum that he must be poor because of his patches, and his silly old sports car, she said that he wasn't poor but that clothes and cars weren't important to him. He must be mad. If I had plenty of money I wouldn't have patches and I would buy a brand new sooooper dooooper sports car. I bet your Christopher has a sooooper dooooper sports car being as he flies jumbo jets.

Love, Max

P.S. This is me with a big fat belly after eating four Easter eggs.

P.P.S. Scallywag stole one of my Easter eggs and was very very sick. Ugh!

17th April

Dear Max,

You're right. Christopher does have a sooooper dooooper sports car, and it terrifies me! When he puts his foot on the accelerator it leaves my stomach behind! I certainly wouldn't like to be kissed by someone with a beard. They're all tickly and full of bits of boiled egg!

If you're going to have scenes in your play with Buster's mum and her fat knight friend, how are you going to get them off the stage before Buster starts chasing the dragon? Remember that if you have a big scene change you might have to have lots of people running backwards and forwards with props, as well as different backdrops and lighting.

I'm doing a radio interview about the film in a few minutes' time so I must fly.

Love D.J.

Dear D.J.,

Mum's gone to the cinema with James.
I wanted to go too, but Mum said the film is
too old for me. Mrs Rabbits is here for the
second day in a row. She started to ask me
about my dad and did I still miss him and she
expected that I would like a new dad and that
Mum must be lonely all on her own. I said
that Mum wasn't all on her own because she's
got me!

Love, Max

P.S. In my play there's going to be a gruesome
ogre that lives under the ground and keeps
popping up to stop Buster from getting to
the dragon.

OGRE: Who's that stomp stomping across my land?

BUSTER: It's me, Buster. I'm going to catch a dragon.

OGRE: Not across my land you're not. All that stomp stomp stomping when I'm trying to watch the telly. Go and catch a dragon somewhere else and stop being a pest.

BUSTER: I wasn't stomp stomping and I'm not a pest.

OGRE: All boys are pests.

24th April

Dear Max,

It sounds as if Mrs Rabbits has rather large feet
and likes to put them in things. Keep that
imagination working, Max, and you'll be able
to magic her out of your house and off into
a field miles away from you! I like the ogre.
Who else is going to pop up in your plot?

Love D.J.

30th April

Dear D.J.,

Mum asked if I mind if James has lunch with us on Sunday. I said I don't, but I do because I like having Mum to myself for Sunday lunch, unless Uncle Derek and Pauline come round. I hope he doesn't stay long because there's a wildlife programme about tigers on the telly, and Mum and I always watch the wildlife programmes together like we used to with Dad. I expect Hairychops won't want to watch it so Mum won't let me either because it would be rude.

Love, Max

P.S. Emily's my other best friend now so I told her about Mrs Rabbits and she gave me a bar of chocolate.

P.P.S. In my play, I'm going to have a bearded knight called Fungus Face who wants to catch the dragon and steal all the glory from Buster.

3rd May

Dear D.J.,

We went to a wildlife park after lunch on
Sunday. Hairychops took us in his silly old
sports car and I sat in this tiny seat
in the back. I was all crunched
up. Mum's hat blew away and
she thought it was really
funny and said at least
it wasn't a wig.
I thought she'd
be upset.

Hairychops doesn't know much about animals,
not like my dad did, so I had to keep telling
him what the animals were. Can you believe
he'd never even heard of a meerkat?! He
bought me a furry raccoon. (He thought it was

a badger!) It's really babyish.
He bought Mum a tiny
bear key-ring and she's
put all her keys onto it.
I think it's stupid.

When Hairychops went
home, he shook hands with
me and said, 'I've learnt a lot, thank you,
Max.' Then he gave Mum another kiss on the
cheek. Yuk!

Love, Max

P.S. Mum recorded the tiger programme so we
didn't miss it. GRRRR!

P.P.S. I did what you said and imagined Mrs
Rabbits far away in a field when she came last
night. She got chased by a fox and fell down
a well. Ha!

10th May

Dear Max,

Poor Mrs Rabbits. Fancy being chased by a fox.

I'm amazed that Hairychops hadn't heard of a meerkat. Even I've heard of a meerkat, and I'm not exactly an expert on wildlife. I soon will be though. Christopher and I have decided to go on safari to South Africa this December, after I've finished *Where There's a Will* and all the fuss about *My Teacher's a Nutcase* has died down. So watch out, Max, I'll be testing you when I come back!

I've just heard that the film of *My Teacher's a Nutcase* is going to be released here on 7th December. They're doing all the special effects at the moment.

Love D.J.

P.S. Do you think Hairychops is hiding something under his beard – like a big mole?!

Dear D.J.,

I think Hairychops is hiding a big family of moles under his beard!

I can't believe you're going on safari! I'd never eat a burger again if it meant I could go on safari! You'll see lions and elephants and crocodiles and hippopottymouses and giraffes and laughing hyenas (yuk!). No tigers though – you can't catch me out there.

I can't wait to see your film. Will we be able to see it where we live? There is a cinema nearby, but it's a bit old and tumblydown and sometimes the film starts to wobble and the music goes all crackly. Or we could go to the big cinema in the middle of town and have popcorn and ice cream but it's a bit expensive.

I asked Mum if Emily could come and see the film with us as well as Ben and Uncle Derek and Pauline and she said yes. So that means you've got six people coming already, which is a good start.

Love, Max

P.S. I'm going to have a princess for Buster to save in my play.

PRINCESS:	Help! Help! O woe is me! I am stuck in my castle and I need to get out to rescue my cat which is stuck up in yonder tree. Please get me down before the dragon returns.
KNIGHT 1:	*(down below)* I cannot help, fair princess. I am too scared of heights.
KNIGHT 2:	*(down below)* I cannot help, fair princess. I'm on my way to a joust.
FUNGUS FACE:	*(down below)* I would help, fair princess, but my beard will catch in the tree.

Dear Max

You're really getting into the spirit of your play. I love the Knight and especially the idea of Fungus Face getting taught in a Tree by his beard. What a Motley Crew! I'm being taken out tonight by the director and producer of 'My Teacher's a Nutcase'. They're going in to help promote the Film. On with the high heels and lippy again.

Love D.J.

P.S. I'm sure 'My Teacher's a Nutcase' will be on at your cinema. I'll find out nearer the time and let you know.

Max
30 Sharpener Street
Anytown
MX9 3BT

Dear D.J.,

Mum's got a big birthday on June 29th. She's going to be 40 and doesn't want to be reminded. Uncle Derek's planning a party for her and Gran and Grandad are coming.

What do you think I should buy her, D.J.? I've saved up a bit of money, but it's not very much. Gran said what about some chocolates, but Mum's on a diet, and Pauline said what about a purse because Mum's old one is tatty. But I want to get her something that tells her I love her and that she's the best. I can't afford a ring, except a plastic one, so what else?

Love, Max

31st May

Dear Max,

Lucky Mum – only 40. Have you thought about buying your mum some flowers, Max? Flowers are a lovely way to tell somebody how much you love them and would make your mum feel very special.

Love D.J.

Dear D.J.,

Flowers are a brillypants
idea, and Pauline agrees.
She said she'd help me
buy them and at the
same time I can
help her choose
her flowers for the
wedding. It made
me feel really
grown-up and
important.

Mrs Rabbits sat last night and I imagined her
with long floppy ears and a fluffy white tail and
a twitchy nose every time she rabbited at me.

I twitched my nose back at her once and she gave me her 'you are really a weird boy' look, then I got the giggles and she said, 'If you're going to be silly you can go to your room.' So I went. Mum was at the theatre club, but at least Hairychops is away for a week, so I've got Mum to myself – YIPPEE!

Love, Max

That's the spirit, Max.
A quick twitch of the
nose works wonders.
I must try it myself
Love D.J.

Dear D.J.

Mum and me went to this **HUGE** park with Uncle Derek and Pauline and Ben. It had a miniature train running right the way round it pulled by a real steam engine. I didn't think the engine would be strong enough to pull Uncle Derek but it did! There were lots of rides to go on as well. We went on the log flumes and me and Ben leaned out so that we got soaked. Then I gave Mum a hug so that she was all wet as well. Ben thinks my family are cool.

Love Max.

P.S. Hairy chops is back the day after tomorrow - Booooo! We have much more fun without him

D.J. Lucas
30 Pencil Drive
Writingdom
DJI OAU

Dear D.J.,

I've been thinking about my play. The fat knight falls asleep and Buster's mum sets off to find Buster. Fungus Face sees her and decides to take her prisoner.

BUSTER: Go home, Mum, and shut all the doors and don't let anyone in except me and the fat knight.

BUSTER'S MUM: I'm scared for us, Buster. What if the dragon carries you away and I never see you again.

BUSTER: Never fear, Mother. That dragon won't get the better of me. I shall fight him with my trusty sword, and if that doesn't work I shall use my frisbee. It is Fungus Face I am afraid of. Don't let him near you.

(In a shady place nearby.)

FUNGUS FACE: I'll soon put a stop to that interfering boy's plans to get rid of me. I'm going to capture his mum and take her miles away across the fields so that he can't find her.

OGRE: You can take her across *my* fields if you wish, Mr Fungus Face. That boy is a pest and needs to be taught a lesson.

(They shake hands and do wicked laughter so that the audience boos.)

Love, Max

P.S. Mrs Rabbit Poo is sitting tonight because Mum's going out for a meal with Hairychops.

18th June

Dear Max,

So your two baddies are going to join forces. What a scary thought! You'll have your audience cowering under their seats. I hope Buster's mum will be all right. Is your big fat knight going to save her, or is Buster going to save his mum from Fungus Face and kill the dragon as well? He's got a busy time ahead of him.

I'm about to nip off to Paris now for two days. My French publisher wants me to do a round of book signings. Paris is my favourite city, so I'm looking forward to it...

Love D.J.

Dear D.J.,

Hairychops was here yesterday. Mum asked
him round for lunch, worse luck. I asked him
how old he was, and he's four years younger
than Mum. (Mum said it was a bit rude but
I thought it was only rude to ask a lady.) He
doesn't look younger with that beard. He looks
YEARS older. He's a bit serious and he asks me
serious questions, but he thinks he's funny.
He's nowhere near as funny as Uncle Derek
or my dad.

When he'd gone, I asked Mum if Hairychops
(I didn't call him that!) was her boyfriend and
she said that she supposed he sort of was.
I didn't know what to say then because I don't

want him to keep coming round because I like having Mum to myself. And if she loves Hairychops she might not love me as much any more. She gave me a big hug though and told me I would always be her number one man, but I don't want there to be another man as well, especially when it means I keep having to have Mrs Rabbits.

Love, Max

Cher Max,

Greetings from Paris, where the sun is shining and the streets are paved with tables and chairs and the smell of strong coffee. I just love sitting at a pavement café and watching the world go by. My hand is stiff from signing hundreds of books - I seem to be quite popular over here.

A bientôt

D.J.

Max
30 Sharpener Street
Anytown
MX9 3BT

Dear D.J.,

I hate Hairychops. Hate him hate him HATE HIM. I gave Mum my flowers and she gave me a big kiss and said they were beautiful and that she loved me very much. Then Hairychops had to go and spoil it. We went to Uncle Derek's for the party, and Hairychops turned up with a HUGE bunch of red roses. I didn't even know he was going to be there, and – you'll never believe it – he had shaved his beard off! It made my flowers look silly, and Mum won't mind if he kisses her now he's a BALDYCHOPS. And if he gave her a huge bunch of roses that means he's trying to pretend that he loves her more than I do, so he's a liar because he can't do because I've known her for ever and he's only just met her.

Now everyone's all upset with me – even Gran and Grandad – because I hid in the cupboard under the stairs so that no one could find me, until Uncle Derek found me, but I didn't want to speak to him or anyone else.

Mum won't love me now and it's all Baldychops's fault. I hate him hate him hate him!

Love, Max

Dear Max,

3rd July

You didn't tell me if there was a big family of moles under Baldychops's beard. I bet there was at least one, poor thing.

Max, I hope you will be feeling better by the time you read this. Have you talked to Pauline about why you were upset? I'm sure she would understand, because she helped you to buy the flowers.

One thing I do know is that your mother will always love you more than anyone else, no matter how many roses they give her.

So chin up, Max, and keep a look-out for those moles!

Love D.J.

Dear D.J.,

Mum had a big chat with me and said I had
upset her very much on her birthday. She
wanted to know what was wrong, but I didn't
know what to say. I just said that someone had
been horrible to me at school and I was in
a bad mood. She wanted to know who, so
I said it was Jenny but that she wasn't to say
anything because it would make things worse.
Now I feel awful because I told a big whopper
to my mum. Jenny deserves it though, because
she's started saying things at school about
Mum having a boyfriend.

I wish Baldychops would just go away and
then things could go back to the way
they were.

At least it's nearly the school holidays. I'm going to Cornwall with Gran and Grandad and Ben's coming with me. At least I won't have to see Baldychops or Mrs Rabbit Poo, but I'll miss Emily.

Love, Max

P.S. There was a mole hiding. It's quite small but I imagine it growing and growing until it takes over his whole face and turns it into a big brown blob.

P.P.S. In my play, Fungus Face captures Buster's mum and with the help of a wicked witch he casts a spell on her to make her think he's the most wonderful knight in all the land.

14th July

Dear Max,

We all tell whoppers sometimes, Max, to
protect people we love. Yours was quite
a little whopper compared to one or two
enormous great whoppers I've told because
I haven't wanted to hurt someone. As long
as it doesn't become a habit. We don't want
your nose growing.

Forget about everything while you're away in
Cornwall, apart from sending me a postcard.
You will not be forgiven if you forget that!

Be brave, Max.

Love D.J.

P.S. There's a seal sanctuary in Cornwall, which you would love. I certainly won't be seeing any seals on my safari.

Dear D.J.,

Baldychops came round for lunch again.
I decided to be nice to him because I didn't
want to upset Mum. He asked if he could read
my play. I didn't really want him to because
I thought he would think it was silly. Mum
persuaded me and, do you know what? He said
he would help me with it if I wanted him to.
I said no thank you very much because you're
helping me and he said in that case I was very
lucky and didn't need him. He did a drawing of
my dragon and he's better at drawing than
sport. Mum showed him some of my drawings,
even though I told her not to, and he said they
were really good but I bet he didn't mean it.

Love, Max

Dear D.J.,

We finished school today. YIPPEE! It's not long till I go on holiday and then it won't be long till Uncle Derek and Pauline's wedding and then it'll be my birthday – and yours. I'm thinking about all the things I've got to look forward to.

Love, Max

P.S. In my play, Buster comes home to see if his mother is all right before going after the dragon again. Fungus Face pretends to be all nice and cuddly, but Buster knows he's faking it because he wants to take his mother prisoner.

FUNGUS FACE: Hello, Buster. How nice to see you. Would you like a toasted crumpet?

BUSTER: I'd like two, please, with butter and honey.

FUNGUS FACE: (to the ogre) Look after our friend, will you?

(Fungus Face goes offstage. Ogre tries to grab Buster.)

BUSTER: Leave me alone, you ugly brute.

(He pushes the ogre into a cupboard.)

That's taken care of her.

(Goes to Fat Knight who is snoring in the corner.)

Wake up, Fat Knight. We've got to get rid of Fungus Face so that Mum will be safe and I can go and fight the dragon.

(The Fat Knight carries on snoring.)

Doh! Then I'll have to do it on my own.

25th July

Dear Max,

He's a feisty little character, your Buster, isn't he? I wouldn't like to tangle with him! Have you thought about asking your friends to act out your play when you've finished it? A play only comes to life when actors jump into the roles and interpret the characters in their own way. I'm sure your teacher would be thrilled if you and your friends were to act it out in front of the rest of the class. That's something for you to think about over the holidays – who should play what part.

I'm flying to New York tomorrow for five days. I'm going to be signing books in bookshops and libraries. It's all part of the publicity for

My Teacher's a Nutty Fruitcake. Between you and me, I'd much rather stay at home and relax in my garden than shoot off to the other side of the world to stay in a boring hotel. Look out for the New York postcard, though I'll be back before it reaches you!

Love D.J.

Dear D.J.,

I know you're not there, but I wanted to tell you that I think your idea about my play is brillypants. I think I'm going to let Ben be Buster. Mum said we could even dress up and she would help with some costumes. Baldychops said he'd help with props, but I said no thank you because my friends would want to do them. Anyway, they'd be Baldyprops! (Get it?)

Mrs Rabbits sat last night. She wouldn't let me watch the football again, so when she went to make a cup of tea, I pulled her knitting off the needles (ha!). She sent me to bed early, but I didn't care because I didn't want to be in the same room as her. As long as she doesn't tell Mum.

I just can't wait to go on holiday now, far away
from annoying rabbits and James the Pain.
I wish I was going to New York like you. That
would be far away enough. I can't wait to add
your New York postcard to my collection.

Love, Max

Dear D.J.,

I'm off on holiday tomorrow — YIPPEE! Ben's staying the night so that we can leave very early, and Uncle Derek is driving us all the way down the motorway to meet up with the wrinklies. (Hee hee, that's what Uncle Derek calls them when no one else is listening!) Uncle Derek says it'll take us hours to get to Cornwall the way Grandad drives, so the earlier we set off the better.

I can't wait for Ben to get here.

I asked Mum if she would be all right on her own because she can't come because she's too busy at work. She said she would find it very very hard and would pine like mad, but she would survive the heartache as long as she knew I was having a wonderful time. And then she said that, seriously, she would miss me but she was sure that James would help her through it. I didn't like that and it made me not want to go because I don't want Baldychops to try and take my place, but Mum said it wouldn't be the same without me so I felt a bit better.

Love, Max

I was here →

Dear Max,

Having a hectic time. I'm being shuttled so quickly from book signing to drinks reception to party that my feet have hardly touched the ground. Christopher's flying in tonight, so I've demanded a night off so we can go and have a quiet meal together, but he's flying straight back to England the next day. New York is amazing. My neck is stiff from looking up at all the skyscrapers!

Love D.J.

Max
30 Sharpener Street
Anytown
MX9 3BT

Dear DJ. My turn to send a postcard.
King Arthur lived in the castle on
the front of this card! Not much
of it left, is there! I might have
a king in my play. He could pay
the dragon a lot of money for
getting rid of Fungus Face because
he doesn't want him in his kingdom.
We went to see that seal sanctuary
you said. It was brilly pants
seeing the seals so close. The hotel's
t a big swimming pool so I have
ces with Ben and he always
ns because he's faster than me
n and Grandad lie by the
ol and Snore.
        Love Max

D.J. Lucas
30 Pencil Drive
Writingdom
DJ1 . OAU

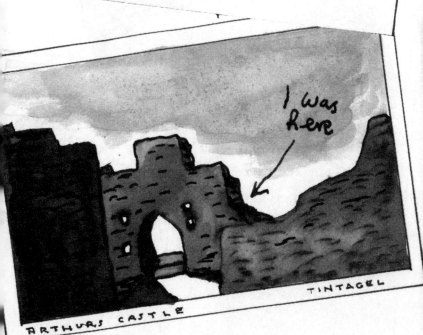

I was here

ARTHUR'S CASTLE   TINTAGEL

Dear D.J.,

I'm back. Did you miss me?! Mum did. When
she opened the door I gave her the biggest
hug in the whole wide world and she gave me
the biggest hug in the whole wide world back.
Baldychops wasn't there, thank goodness.

We had a brillypants holiday. We went to the
beach and we went fishing and Ben and me
tried surfing but we kept falling off. Grandad
said he took my dad to lots of the places we

went to. He said Dad was a pickle because he liked to hide then jump out and shout 'BOO!' Gran said it didn't matter how many times he did it, it always made her jump.
I laughed thinking about Dad doing that, so I did it myself and Gran nearly jumped out of her skin. I told them about my play because I thought my dragon might jump out and say 'BOO!' I said about Mum and the theatre club, but I didn't say anything about Baldychops because I didn't want to think about him trying to take my place.

Everyone's excited about the wedding now. Only three weeks to go.

Love, Max

P.S. Are you going to marry your Christopher? Mum says that's an incredibly cheeky thing to ask, but you don't have to answer if you don't want to.

20th August

Dear Max,

Thank you for your postcard, Max. It sounds
as if you had a wonderful holiday. Your poor
gran, having to cope with one scallywag
after another!

Christopher and I don't have any plans to
get married, but I didn't mind your asking.
We both like being free to scuttle back to
our own shells. When I'm in the middle of
writing a book, I'm probably best left alone
anyway. I can be very grumpy if it's not going
well. Even Donut and Ambush cower in
a corner then.

Love D.J.

Dear D.J.,

Mum's finished my waistcoat and bow tie.
I look a really cool dude in them. This is
a picture of me.

Da Daaa

This is the shortest letter I've ever written
to you!

Love, Max

30th August

Dear Dude

I bet you'll be the coolest dude at the wedding.
Give my very best wishes to Uncle Derek and
Pauline. I hope you all have a fantastic day,
and I look forward to seeing a photograph of
the cool dude.

Love D.J.

Dear D.J.,

Uncle Derek and Pauline's wedding was brillypants. Pauline looked like a film star. It was the first time I'd seen Uncle in a suit. It covered his big fat belly up quite well. I felt very important being with them at the front of the church. Baldychops had to sit behind us with all the Not-So-Important-People (N.S.I.P.s). Ha!

I didn't like the photo bit. It went on and on and on. I was at the top table afterwards at the hotel and Mum let me try some champagne. It was YUK! The bubbles went straight up my nose and made me sneeze.

Baldychops kept putting his arm round Mum, and when they danced together they were all lovey dovey. I don't want him thinking he can marry my mum just because Uncle and Pauline got married. I made Mum dance with me and we did disco dancing with bumping bottoms, not smoochy stuff.

School starts in four days' time. I don't want to go back. We'll have a new teacher, but I want to stay with Miss Dimmer. The new teacher might not let me do my play. I hope I'll be in the football team again.

Love, Max

P.S. I'll send you a photo of the cool dude.

5th September

Dear Max,

It sounds as if the wedding went really well.
You're right about the photo bit. I hate having
my photo taken. Unfortunately, at the moment
everyone wants photos of me. Ah, the price
of fame!

Talking of fame, I've just been invited to
Hollywood to see a preview of My *Teacher's
a Nutcase*. There's a place there called the
Walk of Fame, where the names of famous stars
are etched into star-shaped plaques embedded
in the paving stones. Christopher says he'll
steal out at midnight and etch my name.

I hope your new teacher is even better than Miss Dimmer and encourages you to finish your play and perform it.

Love D.J.

Dear D.J.,

I can't believe you're going to Hollywood! You must be AMAZINGLY famous. Please, please, please will you send me a Hollywood postcard?

I told my friends your idea about doing my play at school. They got really excited and they want to make the props as well, so we don't need Baldychops. Ben can't wait to be Buster and Emily went all pink when I asked her to be the princess. I told Jenny she could be a wicked witch, but she stuck her tongue out at me. I'm going to be the dragon so I can breathe fire over everyone!

I'm in the football team again this term and we've got our first match next week. I'm going to score a million goals and Mum will be watching and she'll cheer like mad because she'll be so proud of me.

Mum's out at the theatre tonight and the Rabbit's coming. I'm going to ignore her and do the final cast list for my play and decide who's playing which part, and I'm going to write a list of the props we need so far.

Love, Max

P.S. Our new teacher is called Mr Hatch, but I call him Eggy in my head because he's quite grumpy. He'd better not stop us from doing my play.

14th September

Dear Dragon,

Watch you don't set fire to your letters!

I'm so pleased all your friends want to be involved in your play. It'll certainly keep you busy if you're going to do all the props and scenery yourselves.

I am really really busy. I'm being rung all the time by newspapers wanting to do interviews with me about the film. A new edition of *My Teacher's a Nutcase* is about to come out with a cover showing the stars in the film – including Tom Trews as the teacher (yes, the inside of the book has had to be changed as well).

I must finish *Where There's a Will* before we go away in December, so back to work…

Have a great birthday, Max. It's worked out that I shall be in Hollywood for my birthday. It all seems incredibly unreal.

Love D.J.

Dear D.J.,

Thank you soooooo much
for my present. I've been
snapping everybody! SNAP
SNAP SNAP! Mum and Uncle
Derek and Pauline bought me
a computer – WHOOPEEEE! – and Uncle
Derek's going to show me how to put my
photographs on it. Mum said that you had
written to check if I would like a camera, so
thank you again, D.J. I'm not going to start
emailing you though. I like writing letters and
I like getting them even more.

Baldychops gave me a set of paints and
brushes and some paper for doing paintings.
Mum says it's the best paper you can get
for painting.

Baldychops and Mum took me bowling with Ben, then we went for a birthday meal. I wish it had been with Uncle Derek and Pauline instead of Baldychops, but they've only just got back from honeymoon. I'm rubbish at bowling, and you'll never believe it but Baldychops was the best, even though he's rubbish at sport. At least he didn't try to hold Mum's hand or anything, because I didn't want Ben to see them.

Love, Max Age 11

P.S. I hope you liked the special card I did for you and that you had a fantastico birthday in Hollywood.

...tings from Hollywood, Max.
...'t believe I've just written
...t! We walked along the Walk
...Fame. There are so many
...mous names from yesterday and
...day, including Tom Trews.
...e film is brilliant, even though
...y've changed lots of things,
...nd everybody thinks it will
...e a big hit.
... hope you had a fantastic
...birthday, and I look forward
...to reading all about it when
...I'm home.

    Love D.J.

Max
30 Sharpener Street
Anytown
MX9 3BT

Dear D.J.,

I hate Jenny Wheeler. She's told everybody
that Mum's got a toyboy and that she saw
them snogging and holding hands like they
were a couple of kids. I said that Baldychops is
only Mum's friend and that they do theatre
together, but Jenny said they do more than
that together and made everyone laugh.
Now it's all horrible again at school. Ben said
I should ignore Jenny because she's always
making trouble, but I didn't want people like
Huge Bigbottom knowing things about my
mum, and I didn't want Emily to think my
mum's a bad person.

Love, Max

Dear D.J.,

I wish Mrs Rabbits would
hop it. She's all yucky
sickly sweet when Mum's
around, but as soon as
Mum goes she turns into
a monster. She got really
cross with me last night
because I wanted to watch
the football on the telly and she
said I couldn't because she wanted
to watch her soap and I said it was my house
so I should be able to choose. She told me off
for being cheeky and said she would tell Mum.

I hate Mrs Rabbits. And I hate Jenny.
And I hate Baldychops because it's all his fault.

Love, Max

1st October

Dear Max,

Jenny's obviously cross because you asked her
to be a wicked witch in your play and not
a princess, so she's trying to hurt you back.
Don't let her, Max. Ben's right. Ignore her.
As for Mrs Rabbits, I suppose she might
believe she had as much right to watch what
she wanted, though I'm hoping the silly old
bat might have felt too ashamed about
making a fuss over a television programme
to tell your mother.

Be strong, Max.

Love D.J.

Dear D.J.,

We've got a match tomorrow and Mum said
she'd watch, but she asked if Baldychops could
come too because he'd like to. I don't want
him to, D.J., because it'll be embarrassing and
they might hold hands. I said to Mum that I like
it when she comes on her own or with Uncle
Derek, and she said but you like James don't
you, so I had to say he was all
right. I didn't want to say
anything else then in
case I upset Mum, but
I think I upset her
anyway because she
said she'd come on her
own but she didn't look
very happy. So I said
I didn't mind if he came,

but I do mind. I'm not looking forward to the match now and I hope I'm not well so that I can't play.

Love, Max

Dear D.J.,

It's all so HORRIBLE. Mum came to watch the match with Baldychops, and Jenny went and stood with them and talked to them. I couldn't concentrate on playing football because I kept wondering what they were saying. Even Ben got cross with me because I kept miskicking the ball. Huge Bigbottom said I was useless and it was my fault that we let in a goal. Then he said, 'Is that your mum's toyboy?' I kicked him, D.J., and I wanted to kick him again and again, but Ben pulled me away. My teacher saw it and sent me off. Mum looked really upset. At the end of the match, Mum and Baldychops started to walk over to me so I pretended not to see them and ran into the school and hid.

We lost the match because of me. My teacher gave me a huge telling off and he's dropped me from the team.

I just want things to be like they were, D.J., just me and Mum.

Love, Max

17th October

Dear Max,

Jenny really has got it in for you, hasn't she, and Huge Bigbottom still seems to be able to make your life miserable, just when you don't need him to be shoving his ugly mug into your affairs. I would have tried to kick him too, Max (though I would probably have missed however big the target), but I would have regretted it afterwards.

Do you think you might talk to Uncle Derek or Pauline about how you feel? No one wants you to be unhappy, especially not your mum, and even James would be upset if he knew he was making you unhappy. Perhaps Uncle Derek or Pauline might be able to talk to your mother for you.

Love D.J.

Dear D.J.,

Mum keeps asking me what's wrong and
I don't know what to say because *everything's*
wrong. I've made her all worried now because
she knows I'm hiding something. She asked if
I wanted her to stay in tonight, but I said I was
fine and that I wanted her to go out.

The Rabbit's here now. I've shut myself in
my room and told her that she can't stop me.
I don't think she cares anyway because her
programme's on the telly.

I'm trying to think about my play so that I can
forget everything else. The gruesome ogre is so
angry at being shut in the cupboard without her
television that she has crashed her way out.
Fungus Face has managed to fool everyone that

he's not really dangerous and only wants to be loved. Everyone wants to be friends with him then, even Buster's friends. When they are left alone, Buster tries to persuade his mother to go with him, but his mother doesn't believe she's in danger because the wicked witch has cast a spell over her.

BUSTER: Fungus Face is up to no good, Mother. (whispering) Believe me, we must get rid of him for good.

BUSTER'S MUM: You're wrong, Buster. He wouldn't hurt a fly.

BUSTER: He's fooling you, Mother. Come with me now, before he can do us any more harm. And while that gruesome ogre is watching the telly.

BUSTER'S MUM: No, Buster, I am staying here. Fungus Face is my friend.

BUSTER: Then I will go and fight the dragon alone and hope that the Fat Knight will wake up and protect you.

(He runs off.)

Love, Max

Dear D.J.,

It's even worse now. Baldychops is directing this
year's Christmas show at the theatre. They've
just started rehearsals and Mum's going to help
do the scenery and costumes. That means she'll
be out with him even more and I'll have to put
up with RABBIT RABBIT RABBIT even more.

Jenny keeps trying to talk to me at school
about Baldychops. She's says he's a bit dishy
and Mum's very lucky to have someone so
dishy, especially since he's younger than her.
And she says her mum says he'll soon get fed
up with having to deal with someone else's kid
when he hasn't got any kids of his own. Or he
might want to have his own kid with my mum
and then I won't be wanted as much. When
she said that, I couldn't help it, D.J., I got hold

of her ponytail and pulled it as hard as I could. Eggy came in when Ben was trying to stop me and he sent me to see the head teacher. Now the head teacher is going to write to Mum.

I'm in such big trouble, D.J. Nobody will want to speak to me now, especially Emily.

I hate everything and I feel like running away.

Love, Max

26th October

Dear Max,

If you run away, where will you run away to?
You'll be cold and scared and hungry, and
you'll have nowhere to sleep and nobody to
talk to. You'll miss your bed and your friends
and your teddy and your mum. Remember
what Buster says in your play: 'Running away
is what cowards do.'

Talk to your mother, Max. She'll be very
upset to know that you've been trying to
cope with your anxieties all on your own.

Love D.J.

P.S. I ran away when I was about your age.
I got as far as the bottom of the road when
a tree made a great creaking noise and sent
me scuttling back home again.

Dear Max,

I'm worried because I
haven't heard from you.
Write soon and let
me know how you are.

Love, D.J.

Dear D.J.,

I ran away, D.J. Mrs Rabbits was sitting and
I packed a bag and sneaked out through the back
door. I forgot my coat and it was raining and it
was dark. I walked and walked and

walked and I kept
thinking that I wanted
Mum, but she wasn't at
home anyway. A big black dog
barked at me and made me jump and
a lorry drove past and splashed me and I wanted

Mum even more, and
Dad too. I wished
Dad was still alive
because then there
wouldn't have been

a Baldychops. I got so wet and cold, D.J., that
I wanted to go home again, but I'd lost my way.

Then a car came up. It was Baldychops's silly old
sports car. Baldychops jumped out and asked
me what I was doing, and I shouted at him, 'Go
away, just go away, it's all your fault.' So he said,
'I will go away, but not until I've taken you home.
Your mother is worried sick about you.' I wanted
her so much that I got in the car. I didn't speak
to him, but when we got to the house
Baldychops said, 'I'd like to be your friend, Max,'
before he drove away.

I just cried and cried when I saw Mum. She gave
me a big cuddle until I stopped, then she asked
me what was wrong, and I told her what they
were saying about Baldychops and having babies
and not wanting me and
being dropped from the
football team, and
Mum cried a bit too
then so I gave her
a big cuddle. She
said I was a daft

duck because I would always be the most important person in her life. Then she said that James was a very nice man and she enjoyed his company, but that it was still early days and that Jenny and her mum were just making mischief. Then I told her about Mrs Rabbits and that I didn't like her – I had to explain who Mrs Rabbits was because I forgot that was my name for her! – and Mum said that was lucky because Mrs Rabbits had a Christmas job and was too tired to sit as well as working.

I feel better because Mum knows now, D.J., but I still wish it was just the two of us.

Love, Max

Dear D.J.,

Mum's been in to see the head teacher and she spoke to Eggy and I think they gave Jenny a big telling off. Emily says she doesn't blame me for what I did because Jenny was being horrible.

I'm going to try really hard to be friends with Baldychops for Mum's sake. I'm going to ask him to help me with my play – I hope you don't mind – and with my drawing. I'll have to hurry up and finish my play now because Eggy – he's all right really – wants us to do it in front of the little ones at the end of term.

Love, Max

10th November

Dear Max,

You sounded so much happier in your last
letter. I'm delighted that Mrs Rabbits has
disappeared back down her burrow. Now that
you're feeling happier, I'm sure you'll race
ahead with your play – especially with
James's help.

I've raced ahead with *Where There's a Will*.
One more chapter to go and it's finished.
I have no idea what I'll be writing about next.
I'm hoping that inspiration will hit me while
I'm leopard-spotting in South Africa. In fact, it
would make a change for me to write about
animals rather than people.

Love D.J.

Dear D.J.,

Why don't you write about meerkats?
Meerkats are amazing. Some of them go
on sentry duty, and some of them act as
baby-sitters! I'd rather have a meerkat
baby-sitting than a rabbit! Uncle Derek and
Pauline have sat the last two times and
Scallywag came with them. He chewed the
nose of the lion mask Mum had made for
Baldychops's play and Mum
wasn't very happy but
I thought it was funny.

Baldychops is coming
for lunch tomorrow.
I'm going to try to
be friendly.

Love, Max

Dear D.J.,

You'll never guess what. Baldychops wants me
to be in his Christmas show! Me! It's called
The Wizard of Oz and he wants me to be
a Munchkin, whatever that is. There's one
Munchkin who has some words to say and
he says I'll be perfect for it. I couldn't believe
he wanted me to be in it, and then I thought
I'd be far too scared. But Baldychops said he
knows from Mum that I'm a big brave boy so
he's sure I can do it.

I said yes, D.J., and I've got to go to rehearsals
on a Saturday afternoon, and Mum's going to
help me learn my lines and make my costume.
Now I've got two plays to work on – my own
and Baldychops's.

Love, Max

P.S. Baldychops did the drawing on the back of this letter. (I didn't want him to know that I call him Baldychops, so I turned it over!) It's what I will look like as a Munchkin.

22nd November

Dear Munchkin,

That's wonderful news, Max. I love *The Wizard
of Oz*, it's such a magical play. You'll have great
fun rehearsing for it. You'll be so busy learning
your lines and finishing your own play that you
won't have time to write to me!

I've finished *Where There's a Will* and I've sent
it off to my publisher. Fingers crossed! Now
I've got to spend the next week touring round
bookshops to sign more copies of *My Teacher's
a Nutcase* before the film comes out. Sadly, I'm
not visiting a bookshop near you, but at least
you've got a signed copy of the book already.

I hope everything's all right at school now.

Love D.J.

P.S. Enclosed with this letter are six tickets
for you and your family and friends to see
My Teacher's a Nutcase at the big cinema in
your town.

Dear D.J.,

Well done, D.J. You've finished it at last! I can't wait to read it.

Thank you sooooooooo much for the tickets. I can't wait! I'm going to take Mum and Uncle Derek and Pauline and Ben, and I'm going to ask Emily but I haven't yet. Mum's going to write to you as well.

I've got a new baby-sitter. She's from Mum's work and her name's Marsha and she says it's all right if I call her Marshmallow. She's really cool, D.J. This is a picture of her.

She likes playing computer games so I've got someone to play with now. (Mum and Baldychops are hopeless at them.) And she's been listening to me say my Munchkin lines and she says she's going to help me make masks for my play (I'm not going to have costumes, except for a tail on the dragon) because Mum and Baldychops are a bit too busy at the moment.

I've nearly finished my play. Fungus Face and the gruesome ogre and the wicked witch are going to be frightened away by Buster riding on the dragon's back.

Buster makes the dragon some toast and Buster's mum comes back from her spell. I want Baldychops to make the dragon mask and he says he will.

I'm going to my first rehearsal on Saturday and I'm really nervous. I hope Baldychops doesn't decide that I'm useless.

Love, Max

29th November

Dear Max,

I'm going to the premiere of My *Teacher's*
a Nutcase in London tonight and I'm petrified.
All the stars will be there, and we have to walk
into the cinema along a red carpet laid out on
the pavement with all the television and
newspaper cameras pointed at us. I've told
Christopher he will have to hold on to me
tightly because I shall probably faint from
fright. I've had to buy a new posh frock, but
I shall probably still look very frumpy alongside
Jennifer Aniseed. Thank goodness we're going
away very soon. At least there won't be any
press on safari.

Wish me luck that my high heels don't catch in the carpet.

Love D.J.

P.S. The new baby-sitter sounds great!

P.P.S. Good luck with the rehearsal, Max.

Dear D.J.,

I saw you on the telly! I was watching it with Mum and Baldychops and suddenly there you were! I crossed my fingers that you wouldn't trip up.

Yesterday I asked Emily if she would like to come to *My Teacher's a Nutcase* with me, and I said that Ben's coming as well. She said she'd love to, and then I wanted to ask if she would be my girlfriend, but that was more scary than standing up in front of everybody. The words just wouldn't come out.

Love, Max

P.S. Jenny still tries to make mischief at school but I just ignore her.

Dear D.J.,

We're going to do my play on the last day of term. I've finished writing it and Baldychops has helped me make a few bits better, and Marshmallow and I have nearly finished all the masks. The dragon mask Baldychops has made is fantastico. I can't wait to wear it. We're rehearsing at school next week with the rest of my friends, and Ben says I mustn't worry what Jenny and Huge Bigbottom think, so I won't.

Love, Max

P.S. The premiere of *The Wizard of Oz* is just after Christmas. I can't wait to walk on the red carpet! Hee! Hee!

8th December

Dear Max,

We're away to South Africa in six days' time.
Congratulations on finishing *Buster and the
Dragon*. I hope you'll send me a signed copy!

I hope you all enjoy *My Teacher's a Nutcase*.
I had a wonderful time at the premiere, even
though I was dreading it. Perhaps I can cope
with being a little bit of a superstar, as long as
I can run away afterwards.

It'll be your turn to be a little bit of a superstar
when you perform *Buster and the Dragon*. And
then you'll be a superstar for a second time in
The Wizard of Oz. You deserve it, Max. Enjoy
every minute of it.

Love D.J.

11th December

Dear D.J.,

Before you go, do you think you might be able
to send me one more ticket for *My Teacher's
a Nutcase*? I know I'm being cheeky, but I think
James might like to come.

Love, Max

Orchard Red Apples

Utterly Me, Clarice Bean	Lauren Child	1 84362 304 8
Clarice Bean Spells Trouble	Lauren Child	1 84362 858 9
The Fire Within	Chris d'Lacey	1 84121 533 3
IceFire	Chris d'Lacey	1 84362 373 0
The Truth Cookie	Fiona Dunbar	1 84362 549 0
Cupid Cakes	Fiona Dunbar	1 84362 688 8
Chocolate Wishes	Fiona Dunbar	1 84362 689 6
The Poltergoose	Michael Lawrence	1 86039 836 7
The Killer Underpants	Michael Lawrence	1 84121 713 1
The Toilet of Doom	Michael Lawrence	1 84121 752 2
The Secret Life of Jamie B SuperSpy	Ceri Worman	1 84362 389 7
The Secret Life of Jamie B Rapstar	Ceri Worman	1 84362 390 0
The Secret Life of Jamie B hero.com	Ceri Worman	1 84363 946 1
Do Not Read This Book	Pat Moon	1 84121 435 3
Do Not Read Any Further	Pat Moon	1 84121 456 6

All priced at £4.99

Orchard Red Apples are available from all good bookshops, or can be ordered
direct from the publisher: Orchard Books, PO BOX 29, Douglas IM99 1BQ
Credit card orders please telephone 01624 836000
or fax 01624 837033 or visit our Internet site: www.wattspub.co.uk
or e-mail: bookshop@enterprise.net for details. '

To order please quote title, author and ISBN
and your full name and address.
Cheques and postal orders should be made payable to 'Bookpost plc.'
Postage and packing is FREE within the UK
(overseas customers should add £1.00 per book).

Prices and availability are subject to change.